I0518250

Nhamo

—First Edition—

Published

By

Edson Mazira

ISBN 978-1-77906-386-1

Nhamo

—First Edition—

© Edson Mazira, 2020

DISCLAIMER

The Story

The story of Nhamo is pure fiction.

Characters

The characters in this book are imaginary.

Places

Every place, including those not mentioned below, is real.

Mash Central

- Chiutsi Village
- Kamutsenzere (Dande Store)
- Mt Darwin Growth Point
- Bindura
- Glendale (Heyshot Farm)
- Mazowe

Harare

- Marlborough
- Mt Pleasant
- Mbare Musika

Masvingo

- Rujeko
- Majange

- Pangolin
- Yeukai
- Gomba
- Sisk
- Mucheke Rank

INTERPRETATION

Foreign words in this book—those that are not English—are interpreted below:

Shona: *Sahwira*

English: This is a mortician (in rural areas) who takes care of the dead body of a person before it is buried.

Shona: *Baba*

English: It's a family title for a father or a husband (Father or Mr).

Shona: *Mai*

English: It's a family title for a mother or a wife (Mother or Mrs).

Shona: *Amai*

English: It's a family title for a mother or a wife (e.g. *Amai Sam* means either the woman who gave birth to Sam or the woman who is Sam's wife).

CONTENTS

CHAPTER 1

NHAMO, a slender Zimbabwean girl with a long innocent face, whose tender skin was very dark, sat cross-legged on a tattered mat in a mud-plastered hut built of Mopani poles. On her thin thighs lay Granny Chihera, a bony old woman with a sunken face whose thin lips were smeared with some sugarless porridge. The old woman was involuntarily spitting it out as she coughed hard, groaning time and again, and that made Nhamo blink out tears through her big eyes.

"Just take this one, *Gogo*," Nhamo persuaded her. "It's the last one, please. You've to eat."

She carefully removed Granny's head from her thighs and made it lie on a pillow. She got up, limped to a mortar bench, where three water buckets were lined up near a shabby wooden shelf packed with old dented utensils, got a cupful of water and poured half of it into a clay pot on a dying fire at the centre of the room. Then, she carried some for Granny to drink.

From the hut, she walked out to a chicken run, where she pulled out two poles from its roof for firewood. The chicken run and the hut were the only buildings standing there. They were located about 100m away from a dust road, which hundreds and thousands of pedestrians and very few vehicles used. Everyone passing by had at least one word to say about Granny Chihera's homestead. The hut, which they used as a kitchen and a bedroom at the same time, once suffered an attack from a whirlwind, so it stood inclined a little to the north, and a stake was diagonally positioned to support it. As for the chicken run, it no longer had fresh chicken wastes.

Nhamo, the poles in her hands, stared at the burnt ruins of a four-roomed house and a round kitchen on a big yard across the dust road. They were surrounded with stunted hedges. The houses belonged to her mother, whose untimely death left her a miserable orphan and forced her to leave school.

"Nhamo!" Mai Soko, their neighbour who lived east, called loudly. "Nhamo!"

"Hello, Granny!" She paced fast towards the hut.

"Hey! Not Granny! It's me here!"

She turned her head. "O Sorry! It's you, Auntie! How's your day?"

"Fine! I'm just worried to see you musing like that! How's Granny?"

"She's fine! Let me attend her!"

"It's okay, Nhamo! Pass my warm greetings to her!"

"Thank you, Auntie!" She walked fast into the hut, carrying the firewood.

"Nhamo, my granddaughter," Granny said in a low voice, "the only child of my late daughter, be of courage in your life. You'll be alone among strangers. You have never known your father. Your mother passed on. You're an orphan.

"The only person who can be patient enough to take care of another person is their mother. The rest can get tired and start complaining."

She threw the poles down. "I can't understand you, Granny." Some tears formed in her eyes, and she rubbed them off with the back of her right palm. "I won't be alone; you can't leave me. I'm only 14 years old."

"I can't make it, my grandchild."

"What does that mean, Granny?" She walked and crouched near her.

Her reply was nothing other than a unique cough whose hem was some deadly silence that caused much tears to race down Nhamo's cheeks.

"I'm still waiting for the answer, Granny." She paused for some seconds. "Can't you hear me, eh? Answer your granddaughter, please! Granny Chihera! Granny! Chihera! Chi..." She shook her, checked her pale eyes and felt her pulses.

A sharp scream broke out of the hut and sounded like the one of a referee's whistle calling out twenty-two players to march into a soccer field. One by one, or in companies of two or three, all female neighbours hurried to Granny

Chihera's home, tying their doeke and wrapping their waists with multicoloured cloths. Their husbands watched anxiously from distant places until their wives beckoned at them to come close.

Nhamo and the women wept so loudly that almost everyone in Chiutsi Village heard them. The bad news spread like waves on a disturbed lake. A number of village workmen could be seen going back home with their tools, yoked oxen or donkeys pulling ploughs or carts, and so on. It was a taboo to continue with work when there was such misfortune. The number of the mourners increased a little as people from neighbouring villages fell in from different directions, holding plates and dishes full of mealie-meal. Two big fires were made, one for the men and the other one for the women to cook some food and also to warm themselves.

Although Granny was a very social person, very few mourners could be seen around her home.

"This is pathetic. Look at how embarrassing it is," blurted out Matumbu, a village mortician, s*ahwira* as they called him in their native language, *Chishona* or *Shona*. "Only two people have attended this funeral. It's because you're poor." His index finger pointed at Granny's dead body wrapped in a brown blanket. "If you'd a kraal with at least one cow, even a calf, hundreds and thousands of people would be here. They like to eat meat too much. Greedy villagers. Whose funeral did you, Chihera, not attend in this village of Chiutsi? You even attended the funerals in the neighbouring villages—Chihota, Katarira, Kapfudza, Chisanhu, Seya, Bhinya Road, and so on. You wept with them when they wept; you always stood with them in times of trouble. Today is your turn; they forget you. Bad people. Good-for-nothing friends.

"Maybe you're a witch; they're afraid of your killing goblins. Yeah, this is true." He slowly turned to Nhamo and looked her in the eyes. "How dare you mourn for a dangerous witch?"

The grieved girl freaked, snatched a mug with homemade beer from Matumbu's left hand and hurled it away. She slapped him and spat in his face before Mai Soko stopped her. Everyone blamed the mortician for his scathing comments. Although it was cultural for any traditional mortician to utter any words of their interest, Matumbu's last comment was a sharp thorn piercing in the centre of everybody's heart. Some elders dragged him by the hand and went with him behind the hut. There, they took a few minutes, talking. Gestures could tell from afar that they were reprimanding him.

Sometime later, soon after everyone had taken their supper, a large number of young people from the village clustered at the centre of the yard, dancing to drumbeats yielding a cultural tune named *jiti*. Two people at a time—a boy and a girl—were given some minutes to dance within a ring created by singers and drumbeaters. The girl danced in such a way that she shook her figure in front of the boy who sometimes pretended as if he wanted to touch it, but that was done with caution because touching it always attracted a big slap or a blow in the face usually followed with some hysterical laughter and mockery from the spectators.

Nhamo leered at them. *They're happy because my granny is dead. Instead of mourning with me, they're dancing. When my mother died, they did the same.*

At around 2 a.m., the boys and the girls retired to bed and left their elders warming themselves by the fires.

"It's time for *katekwe!*" Baba Soko, Granny's neighbour, shouted, seated by the fire. "The kids who've been making us remember the days of our youth have left us!"

Everyone nodded; the women ululated. They all rose and formed two parallel lines, one for the women and the other one for the men, both of which were perpendicular to the one of the drumbeaters, and there was a distance of about ten metres between them. Standing in that manner, they began to sing. One male left his friends singing, danced towards the women and selected one lady with whom he danced back to the males' line where she selected a new male dancer. With him, she danced back to the females' line where the man chose a new female dancer to accompany him back to his line. The dance went on like that until their clothes were soaked in sweat.

Some hours later, a new old sun was spat out by the eastern horizon to witness the burial of the old woman. By that time, a grave had already been dug at Muuyu Graveyard, the graveyard located in the east of Chiutsi Village, which was named after a huge hollowed baobab tree planted in it.

"Brave men, welcome back from the land of the dead where every night is a night of strange firecrackers in the air!" Matumbu applauded eight men carrying peaks, axes and shovels as they approached Granny's home. "How deep is my girlfriend's new room?"

"It's deep enough for her to rest in peace," one of the men answered smilingly.

Baba Soko joked: "Matumbu couldn't do it, haha! Going to Muuyu Graveyard between 2 a.m. and 4 a.m. is not for the faint-hearted cockroaches like you, Sahwira Matumbu. These warriors started digging at around 4 a.m. when you were snoring by the fire here."

"Get away, Soko! I fear nothing; I'm a smart person. Ghosts have absolutely nothing to do with a person who doesn't use *juju*. I'm Matumbu 'Special.'"

"Haha, cease fire!" Baba Soko lifted up a wooden stool and went to sit near his wife.

Matumbu followed the gravediggers, blurting. "I know it. They've kept aside 5litres of beer for you. I'm not going to leave you."

A certain lady commented as she walked past Matumbu, "Why do you always think about beer?"

In the hut, Matumbu's wife—a character that never spent much time talking to people—was, on behalf of her husband, taking care of the dead body. At around 2 p.m., she bathed it and clad it with a white sheet before four men carrying a ladder-like wooden structure got in.

Some minutes later, there was much mourning as the men carried the dead body out of the hut. Mai Soko and two other women remained in the room, fanning Nhamo with a winnower. They rubbed her feet with salt and poured water onto her head, while she lay unconscious on the floor.

"Nhamo!" Mai Soko called into her left ear. "Nhamo!"

One of the other women suggested: "Don't call her name; call the name of her grandmother."

"I don't know her first name."

"Just say Chihera."

"Chihera!" she called once into the left ear and twice into the other one, "Chihera! Chihera!"

Nhamo woke up and heard a familiar song:

Aenda waenda, haachadzoki!

Aenda waenda, haachadzoki!

Aenda waenda, haachadzoki!

The song went on like that. It simply meant that Granny Chihera had gone for good.

CHAPTER 2

AFTER the burial, Baba Soko and Mai Soko took Nhamo to their home.

"Nhamo"—Mai Soko, seated under the veranda of her main house, comforted Nhamo—"since you say this village is no longer comfortable for you, Pastor Soko, my son, will live with you in Harare.

"You're now part of our family. Feel at home."

"But why did God do this to me?" Nhamo asked, unable to contain herself. "It started with the death of my mother; some enemies burnt her in her house. Now, it's my grandmother... I don't know the face of my father. Why me? Why?" Tears ran down her tender cheeks.

Touched, Mai Soko said, "Sorry, Nhamo. Such is life. This God is the god of the orphans and the widows. He loves them very much."

"Does He?"

"He does," she said, nodding fast.

At that time, a Kukura-Kurerwa bus halted at Munanga Bus Stop. The villagers—the children and the adults—as their norm, ran to the bus stop and stood around. They had different missions. Some had come to find out if their relatives had visited them. Others—especially the male adults—always came to carry the visitors' luggage for a few dollars to buy *kachasu* beer. The little boys usually wanted to study the bus so that they could make their own wire toys.

"See, Ringson," one of the little boys shouted, "the seats of a bus face forward, not backward. You have to destroy your toy bus and make a new one."

The people on the bus who got what the little boy was saying laughed.

Pastor Soko, stepping down from the bus, said smilingly, "Little boy, go and get Mai Soko for me. That's the punishment for picking on your friend."

The little boy sprinted to call Pastor Soko's mother, who quickly came pushing a wheelbarrow to carry her visitors' luggage.

The bus left the bus stop. Tasvi, a known drinker in Chiutsi Village, helped Mai Soko push the wheelbarrow loaded with cartons. He knew quite well she would give him something in return.

Nhamo welcomed the visitors. She took the luggage into the main house; meanwhile, Mai Soko prepared places for them to sit.

Baba Soko just arrived from herding his cattle. "Son, welcome." He diagonally placed his axe against the wall. "I saw cocks fighting this morning before I went out into the forest. They were actually foretelling about your visit."

Pastor laughed. "Really?"

"Sure!" They shook hands. "How do you do?"

"How do you do?"

Pastor's wife walked out of the house and greeted her father in-law. She sat on a mat near her husband's chair.

Baba Soko looked around in surprise. "Where are they? My grandsons."

"We didn't bring them," Pastor joked.

"Don't try my temper." He faked anger and looked at his daughter in-law. "My in-law, I know you always tell me the truth."

"They're inside with their *Gogo*," she said.

Baba Soko sprang up and dashed into the house. He came back with them and let them sit on his thighs. "My good friends, how's Harare?"

"It's fine"—the younger boy blurted out—"but next month we'll shift to Glendale."

His parents looked at each other and laughed.

Baba Soko laughed, too. "Really? Who told you all this?"

"Daddy...Mama."

"Are you happy with that?"

"No."

"Why?"

"I don't want to leave my toy."

"You'll just carry it with you. That won't be a problem, my grandson."

Everyone laughed.

Baba Soko's neighbours came, one by one, to greet the visitors. They chatted, but one person was missing. Had God not called her, she would have been the first one of the neighbours to greet them. Granny Chihera.

The sun motioned and slid into the pocket of the western horizon.

"The sun's gone. I'm leaving for my home; my eyes won't cope with the dusk." One of the neighbours stood up.

"No! You can't go." Pastor blocked him. "Everyone must take supper with us. I'll accompany everyone to his doorstep."

He obeyed him.

CHAPTER 3

ON the day of her journey to Harare, Nhamo was in high spirits. She could not stop looking at herself from her feet up to her bosom. For the first time in her life, she was wearing her own new shoes and had cat-walked all the way from home to the bus stop. Here and there, she lifted up her legs to check the soles. Baba Soko and Mai Soko secretly laughed at her as they waited for the second bus to come. The first one had passed by too early—at around 1 a.m.

Baba Soko asked, "How many buses went to Mukumbura yesterday?"

"Four," Mai Soko said. "I heard them pass by.

"Listen!" She paid attention. "That's a bus."

The others paid attention, too. Nhamo smiled. Some minutes later, a truck with cattle passed by, and it swept away Nhamo's smile.

Baba Soko picked on his wife: "That's your ancestors' bus, isn't it?"

Ignoring her husband, she said, "Next time you won't stay for a short time like what you've done, my in-law."

"Sure, Mama. Next time I promise to stay for at least a month," said she.

Pastor said, "I am sure that one is a bus."

Baba Soko nodded. "Yeah."

Nhamo smiled. *This time, we're gone.*

Mai Soko said, "Maybe it's another truck."

Pastor said, "That sound is not of a truck."

Baba Soko chipped in, looking at his wife: "Engines of vehicles are not pots and plates; men know them, but women don't know them."

The bus showed up. Baba Soko could study it from Munanga Bus Stop. Its headlights showed it was a bus, not a truck as Mai Soko had said it. There was no doubt at all. Nhamo's smile increased and touched her ears. Baba Soko waved for it to stop. The bus stopped.

"Goodbye!"

"Goodbye. Safe journey!"

"Thank you!"

Nhamo tottered as the bus began to move before she sat down. She gripped the seats, confused. Every passenger stared at her. Pastor directed her to move forward, but she hesitated. Mai Pastor overtook her and led her to the back seat. She followed her, unsteady, trembling. Her face was heavy. She could not look up to face the other passengers; neither could she do it to face Pastor nor his wife.

She sat by the left window and tried to peer through it. Nothing could be seen outside, except another Nhamo being reflected in the window, another Mai Pastor, another Pastor Soko and the other boys—their sons.

The bus parked at Dande Store in Kamutsenzere for so long until the morning sun showed its rays. Now, Nhamo could see everything outside. She felt uneasy when she caught sight of some words inscribed on a building: NHERERA BATANAI. The words simply meant 'ORPHANS, BE UNITED'.

The bus conductor apologised: "The bus is now in good condition. Our mechanics have repaired it. We are sorry for the inconvenience. Let's go now."

They crossed over Mavuradonha Mountain. A lot on the way drew Nhamo's attention. Trees seemed to be racing outside. Women were going to fetch water. Cattle were grazing near the road. Children were going to school. Mavuradonha Boarding School was at her right side; she looked at it when Pastor mentioned it. A cart with donkeys carried vegetables and tomatoes and was parked near a baobab tree.

At Dotito Growth Point, two little boys wearing dirty, torn school uniforms were selling mangoes around stationary buses. They wore no shoes, and it looked as if the boys had no relationship with bathing water. Unkempt hair. Yellow teeth. Eye rheum. Feet chaps. Nhamo understood the boys were as poor as she was. Maybe they were orphans, too. A policeman walked near them, and they ran away, but he seemed not to care about them; he just concentrated on his walking up to a nearby police station. Two female police officers bought bananas from a stout woman seated on a bucket. Mai Pastor bought a bottle of coke and a packet of biscuits from an old man, who had just boarded the bus to sell his stuff. There was a lot of activity.

The bus left the rank, but it ranked again at Mt Darwin Growth Point, but for a short time now. It set off and ranked in Bindura. Nhamo stood up to get down because Mai Pastor had also stood up from the seat.

"Where to?" Mai Pastor asked, arcing her eyebrows.

"Isn't this Harare?" Nhamo answered with a stunning question.

"This is Bindura. Bindura Musika. Rank."

"Ok." She sat down, shamefaced.

Some passengers laughed hysterically. Others considered it and felt sorry for the girl.

After sometime, they left Bindura. Later, Mai Pastor shook Nhamo's right leg. "See. That's Glendale. To your right side."

She looked up but did not see it clearly because of the other passengers on their seats.

"Next month," said Mai Pastor, "we'll shift from Harare to this place."

"Ok."

In Mazowe, a place popularly known for growing oranges, just after Glendale, the bus stopped at a roadblock near Mvurwi Turnoff. Sergeant Zhira of Glendale Police Station stepped up and began to check the passengers' national IDs. Upon seeing him, Nhamo's stomach churned. The police officer was tall and dark in complexion. His eyes were a bit big. He walked to the back seat and checked Pastor's and Mai Pastor's IDs. Before he left, he cast his suspicious eyes unto a white bucket positioned between Pastor's legs.

"Can I search in your bucket, sir?" he asked with a bold voice.

"It's goat meat"—Pastor opened the bucket for him—"from Chiutsi Village. Mukumbura."

"I see. Do you have papers permitting you to move with this carcass?"

"No. My parents just killed it for me. I'm a pastor," he said politely.

"Is that the answer to my simple question?"

"Sorry. No papers."

"Get down with your bucket now!"

Pastor did not hesitate. He quickly gripped the bucket and stood up. "I'm sorry, Officer."

"Is this your family?"

"Yes, sir," he said, nodding sheepishly. "My wife. My two kids. My neighbour's daughter." He lowered his voice: "She lost both her mother and her granny. Never known her father. I now take her as my daughter."

The policeman looked at the girl. "What's your name?"

"Nhamo." She swallowed her saliva after saying it.

"Mister, give me your full details," the sergeant demanded, fishing out a police notebook and a pen from his pocket. "Give me your national ID again."

The pastor handed the ID over to him.

"Make sure this meat is not from a stolen goat. I know your area has too many stray goats."

"I'm honest, sir."

"Sign here."

The pastor signed in the notebook.

"It's okay."

"Thank you."

Sergeant Zhira walked out.

One of the passengers commented: "You're lucky, chap. That policeman doesn't forgive people. I've known him for quite a long time."

"Really? So I praise God."

"Not now. Better praise Him after you win the Marlborough police roadblock. That's a *dandemutande*, a spiderweb," the man said and sipped some beer from a container he had fished out from his satchel.

"It's okay," the pastor said and remained silent. He had observed the man was drinking secretly.

At Marlborough, the police waved the bus to pass through the roadblock.

The drinking man said, "Jah God has special favors for pastors. When I grow up, I want to be a pastor."

A woman seated next to him asked, "How old are you now?"

"50."

The passengers around him laughed.

The bus stopped at Mt Pleasant, a low density suburb in Harare, just after Marlborough, another low density suburb also in Harare. Pastor and his family disembarked.

CHAPTER 4

"THIS is your new home in Harare, Nhamo," Mai Pastor said, looking at Nhamo. "This place is called Mt Pleasant."

Nhamo just gaped at the spacious room doubling the size of her granny's hut. The furniture in it—the shiny leather sofas and so on—had grabbed her mind.

Mai Pastor shook her, Nhamo's, shoulder. "Hey!"

"Sorry?" She looked at her, alarmed.

"Don't worry about all these things. This is your home; you've much time to study them."

She nodded sheepishly.

"Let's move around. I want to show you a few things necessary for a visitor."

They got up and toured around in the yard.

"Next week, I'll take you to the heart of Harare before we shift to Glendale."

"Is Glendale in Harare?"

"No, it's out of Harare. You didn't notice it?

"But we have Greendale in Harare. The difference between the two lies on *Gree* and *Gle*."

"Ok." *Glee and Gle. Glee and Gle...* She repeated it in her mind.

They came back and sat in the lounge. Nhamo's eyes got stuck to the screen of a big TV. Attentively, she sat inclined towards it as if she wanted to spring up like a cat.

Mai Pastor got up silently and walked to the kitchen. Pastor was in the master bedroom, reading his books. The kids were playing with toys outside the house. Nhamo, when she noted later she was alone, stood up, walked to the TV and tried to peep into it.

Mai Pastor came back and coughed behind her. "There're no people inside." She laughed.

Nhamo smiled, embarrassed, and walked back to where she was seated.

"Take this food." She handed her a lunchbox with fresh potato chips and a large piece of chicken.

"Thank you, Auntie."

"Call me Mama. And Pastor Daddy. You're our daughter. These little boys are your brothers."

"Ok."

"Feel at home."

"Thank you."

A week later, Mai Pastor took Nhamo into town. Nhamo's clumsy actions attracted many people. She stopped and stared at shop dummies wearing clothes until Mai Pastor pulled her.

They reached Mbare Musika.

"This is Mbare," said Mai Pastor. "This is the biggest flea market in Harare. You get almost everything in this place. Too much activity here."

Nhamo said nothing; instead, her stomach began to churn. She had heard much of Mbare before she physically set her feet on it. According to the stories she had heard from many people in her rural, Mbare was a place of rogue people— thieves, robbers, crooks, gringos, and so on. Because of that, she disliked it.

A tall man with dreadlocks approached them, touting: "Mukumbura! Mukumbura! The bus just needs one passenger! Are you going?"

"We're not," Mai Pastor replied.

"Does he know us?" asked Nhamo.

"No."

"But he mentioned Mukumbura when he saw us."

Mai Pastor smirked. "I'll explain it to you when we get home." She yawned.

"Ok."

"Masvingo! Beitbridge..."

"Freezits! Eggs..."

"Cellphone chargers! Toothbrushes..."

"Dollar for five! Get cheap sweets! Mints! Toffees! Special offer..."

"One *asara*! One..."

"Mukumbura via Mt Darwin! Bindura..."

"*Hodha bhero*! Jean trousers! T-shirts! Shoes..."

"Screen guard, phone *yese*! Screen guard, phone *yese*! Screen guard..."

Different voices were shouting. Nhamo now understood why the tall man had approached them.

CHAPTER 5

A NEW old sun cast its rays onto the locations of Glendale, a new home for Pastor and his family.

Nhamo was over the moon that she had left Mt Pleasant with the knowledge of Harare City. Now, she could go alone without the company of another person.

"This is Westview"—Mai Pastor told Nhamo—"a medium density suburb in Glendale. I don't know much about it, but I hope Deaconess Mercy, one of our church members, is coming this morning to drive us around it."

"Ok, Mama."

At around 7 a.m., Deaconess Mercy arrived, carrying some groceries in her car. She received a warm welcome fully packed with smiles and hugs.

Immediately, Brother Sam arrived on his bicycle, a 5litre container of fresh milk tied to the carrier. He was from Heyshot Farm.

Sometime later, Mercy and Nhamo went into the kitchen to prepare some food for breakfast. Sam moved around the yard, weeding flower beds. Pastor and Mai Pastor sat on their chairs, basking in the sun.

"I'm Mercy Mbezo," Mercy told Nhamo. "I'm a teacher of English language at Rujeko High School. The school is at Rujeko location, where I stay. It's here in Glendale."

"I'm Nhamo." She stopped what she was doing to explain. "I'm an orphan. Now, I don't have even a single person to call my relative. My mother was burnt in her house. My grandma died recently. I don't know my father. I'm a bastard in fact." Her eyes blurred with tears.

Mercy hugged her. "It's ok, Nhamo. I love you."

"Grandma told me my father was a policeman. He met my mother when she was working at a farm called Heyshod. I don't know where the farm is."

"Heyshod or Heyshot?"

"I don't really know."

"If it's Heyshot, the farm is here in Glendale. That's where Brother Sam, the boy outside, stays. It's just three farms from here. Not far. You go past Dutch Farm, Boroma Farm and Kahuku Farm. Heyshot is opposite Kilmer Farm. I usually go there to buy farm produces."

"Really?"

Mercy nodded. "If your father is a policeman, he may be working at Glendale Police Station opposite Valley Section shops. I'll show you the station some other time. Maybe he's still there. Do you know his name?"

"No."

"Hmm. Challenge. Anyway, according to God's will, you'll meet him one day."

"Let it be so."

When the breakfast had been served, they sat down and ate. After it, they all chatted under the veranda of the house. The sun was hot.

"Where does that main road go?" Pastor asked.

Brother Sam replied, "Concession. Via White Cliff."

"Ok."

Many church members visited them. Each had a present for them. Those who failed to come that day came the following day and so on.

One night, when Brother Sam was at his home, he found it hard to sleep on his bed. He sat up and leaned on the wall. His mind was busy: *I'm sure she's the right one for me. I must marry her.*

"Nhamo, I love you," I'll say.

"Me too," she'll reply.

Now, how shall I approach her? Should I tell Deaconess Mercy? Elder Dube? Pastor? Mai Pastor? Who?

In the morning, his mother called, "Sam!"

"Hello, Nhamo. Ah, sorry, Mama."

"Time's up for work. Are you not feeling well?"

"I'm well." He sprang up and haphazardly put on his overall and his gumboots.

"Come for some porridge first."

"No appetite."

She arced her eyebrows. "For the first time... What's the matter?"

"No problem."

"Umm."

He left home.

At night, he did not take his supper properly. His stepfather Matumbu, who had visited them all the way from his rural home in Chiutsi Village, noticed it and was moved within his heart.

He complained: "Son, your mood is strange. It seems you're not happy with my visit."

"No, Baba. I'm—"

"Maybe you don't like the goat meat I brought you, eh? I thought you would enjoy it as usual."

Sam's mother, Matumbu's side chick, chipped in: "He's been like this since morning. His mood is also eating me up. My BP is shooting up. Let me die and leave him alone.

"He refused to take his porridge in the morning. *No appetite* was his response."

"Look, you're now worrying your mother. What's your problem?"

Sam felt sorry for her mother and decided to let the cat out of the bag. He drooped his head. "I want to marry."

There was a wave of silence for a moment. Matumbu broke it and said, "That's not an issue, is it? Can that make a person who wants to be a father get worried? Did your mother deny it? Did you tell her about it?"

He shook his head; meanwhile, his mother shrugged.

Matumbu smiled. "Where's my daughter in-law?"

"Westview, Glendale."

"For how long have you been in love?" He stroked his beard.

"I've not yet proposed..."

Another wave of silence struck them. It was heavier than the first one.

"This is madness!" his mother insulted and stood up. She left them and went to sit by the fire in the kitchen.

Matumbu patted him on the back. "Take it easy. Approach her first. I promise, you're going to win her. After that, you'll talk about marriage. Not now.

"What's her name?"

"Nhamo. She's nice."

"It's ok. Nhamo is yours."

The name did not click in Matumbu's mind that the girl was Granny Chihera's granddaughter, Nhamo, the orphan.

In the kitchen, Amai Sam complained: "He's immature! How can he behave like that over a flying bird not in his cage? 'No appetite.' 'No appetite.' What a stupid boy!"

"It's ok, *Masibanda*!" Matumbu's voice rose. "Forgive my son!

"Son, don't wrong your mother again by not eating your food because of such minor issues. Feel free to share them with her."

He nodded.

"It's over," Matumbu concluded. "Let's discuss other things."

CHAPTER 6

THE other night, it rained cats and dogs. Nhamo and the kids were in one of the spare bedrooms. She was awake, trying to make out what Pastor and Mai Pastor were arguing about in the master bedroom. The rumbling thunder and the rain pattering on the corrugated asbestos of the roof were pissing her off—they were obstructing her from grasping the argument that seemed to involve her, Brother Sam and Deaconess Mercy.

Sam had preached well in the afternoon; Deaconess Mercy had encouraged the congregants to pledge and give groceries, money, and so on to their new pastor. Nhamo had done nothing, so she wondered why she was also being discussed in the room.

The rain ceased abruptly, and the noise dwindled, but a number of frogs had started their band somewhere outside. However, their noise was not as disturbing as that of the rain and the thunder. Now, she could make out Pastor's and Mai Pastor's arguing voices.

"Nhamo is too young to get married! Period!" That was Pastor's angry voice. "She's 14. What'll the people of my village say if they hear she's married? What type of a pastor will they think I am?"

"Do you live for the people or for God? Why do you've to worry about what they'll say? People are people; they were born to speak whatever rubbish they want.

"Until what age, then, do you want to take care of this orphan? Tell me!"

Pastor remained silent, but he frowned and leered at her.

"Many farm girls get married at her age."

"Is she a farm girl?"

"She's an orphan."

Nhamo sobbed in her room. The whole night, she did not sleep. She just sat on her bed, tears and mucus flowing down her face.

In the morning, Pastor left home for a popular prayer mountain in Bindura, a town located about forty kilometres away from Glendale. Mai Pastor, Nhamo and the kids were left alone.

When Pastor had hit the road, his wife got an opportunity to discuss with Nhamo.

"Nhamo," she called, walking out of the lounge.

"Mama," she answered from the kitchen.

"Follow me to the veranda."

She stopped her chores and followed her.

"The weather is fine." Mai Pastor looked up and around. "Get two garden chairs."

Nhamo got them.

"The other one's for you." She grabbed hers. "Before you sit down, get us cold drinks."

The girl went inside and came back holding two bottles of coke.

"Give me one. The other one's for you."

"Thank you, Mama"

"Don't mention it."

They sipped for a moment without talking.

Mai Pastor broke the silence and asked, "Do you know Brother Sam?"

"Yes, I know him, Mama."

"He preached very well yesterday, didn't he?"

"Yes, he did."

She cleared her throat and sipped from her bottle. "He's a nice brother I took my time to study. Deaconess Mercy told me much about his perfect life." She paused and looked at Nhamo, who was just quiet—not even sipping her drink. "He sent Deaconess Mercy with some good news for you. He loves you to be his future wife. I don't despise this. My spirit is ministering unto me that this is your future hubby, who'll change your life.

"Can you accept his proposal?"

She shook her head. "I'm too young to get married, Mama."

Mai Pastor cackled. "At what age do girls get married?"

"After 18."

"Don't be ridiculous. Don't compare yourself with those girls whose lives are perfect. They've parents, and they're going to school. Don't forget you're an orphan, you're not going to school, and so on. This is your chance to change your life."

Nhamo's heart was moved enough to drive out her tears.

"Do you see me and my family?" she asked rhetorically. "I got married when I was 35. At this age, I'm a mother of two little kids. This is not good for my age.

"You need to be very careful. Fortunes come once in a blue moon. Many girls are getting married at your age."

"I don't like it, Mama; I'm too young."

"Get out of my sight now! Go and wash all the utensils including those we've not used. After that, get a hoe to dig in the garden. All this must be done in thirty minutes because there's a lot of work awaiting you. Go! What're you still waiting for?"

Nhamo walked away, tears forming in her eyes. She remembered her granny's words: *"The only person who can be patient enough to take care of another person is their mother. The rest can get tired and start complaining."*

Mai Pastor followed her to the kitchen. "Why're tears on your cheeks? Have I done wrong to ask you to wash the utensils? A lazy girl! You need to be grateful! You're now a burden on my shoulders! Please, I'm not the one who killed your mom and that poor crone you called *Gogo*! I need some space! This is not an orphanage to take care of lazy orphans like you!"

Nhamo burst into a pitiable cry.

"Cry louder than that if you want to! I don't care about it at all!"

"Don't do this to me, Mama," she pleaded miserably.

"Do I look like your dead mother? Don't you mock me. I'm a mother of two, not of three. Understood?

"Sob and work. The two must go hand in hand."

Nhamo washed the utensils and dried them with a towel. She went out to a mango tree and took a hoe hung on a branch. The hoe on her right shoulder, she walked to a vegetable garden in front of the house and began to dig mixing the soil with some manure. She had never worked like that before. Her hands ached. She worked until sweat soaked her dress.

Mai Pastor followed her again and gave her another task of emptying two big plastic bins. The bins were heavy, but Nhamo had no choice.

She got a wheelbarrow and loaded one of them onto it.

"Little knowledge!" She sneered. "What do you want to throw away, the litter or the bin?"

"The litter."

"So why do you load the bin onto the wheelbarrow?"

She did not answer back.

"You lack common sense! Just offload the litter into the wheelbarrow and leave the bin alone!"

She did so.

"Now, drive the wheelbarrow across that main road and dump the litter. Do it fast because I want you to cook some food for me. You're not using my stove today; you've to make a fire out of those wet pieces of firewood over there."

Nhamo dumped the first load and then the second one. On her way from the dumping site, she came across Sergeant Zhira, the police officer she once saw at the roadblock, when she was going to Harare for her first time.

"Good afternoon, sir."

"Afternoon," his voice vibrated. "It looks as if you want to tell me something." He narrowed his eyes and looked her straight in the eyes. "What's it?"

"I...," she hesitated when she saw Mai Pastor staring at her over the durawall. "Nothing, sir." She swallowed her saliva.

"Sure?"

"Sir."

The policeman shrugged and moved on.

Nhamo secretly turned her head to see where the man was going. She saw him enter the third durawall from theirs.

Mai Pastor, her hands on her hips and her right foot tapping on the ground, welcomed Nhamo with a question as she entered the yard: "What did you tell the officer?"

She stopped, the wheelbarrow still in her hands. "Nothing."

"You don't appreciate, Country Girl. I showed you town life all the way from your rural home. You were used to bathing with no soap, to eating junk food, to sleeping on the ground, to wearing tattered clothes, and so on. Now, you've relaxed and forgotten your past."

Nhamo began to sob.

"Go and make the fire before I hit you in the face!"

Nhamo pushed the wheelbarrow and positioned it under the mango tree. She went to make the fire outside the house and then cooked the food. The food was half cooked because of the wet pieces of firewood.

"You're wasteful, Miss Orphan. I didn't know you're a witch. You've done this intentionally, right?"

"The fire—"

"Shut your stinking beak, Vulture!" She charged towards her. "I don't want to hear anything about the fire!

"Right now, eat all this half-cooked food; I'm watching you."

"Mama, this is too much," she begged. "It'll make me sick."

"Who cares? Don't test my temper, Miss Orphan."

She ate it all and began to vomit. "I now want to get married, Mama."

She smiled. *Done.*

The 14-year-old girl wiped her mouth with the back of her left hand. Her eyes were red and wet with tears. Her head was covered with sweat.

"This marriage will be good for you, my daughter. I'll convince Sam to send you to school. These days, we've many private schools offering lessons to school droppers.

"Go and take a shower, my lovely daughter." She helped her get up.

After bathing, Nhamo went to bed. Although it was still day, she deserved some rest.

CHAPTER 7

"TODAY," Mai Pastor said to Nhamo, both of them seated under the veranda, "Pastor is coming back from Bindura. What happened yesterday is for the two of us, right?"

Nhamo nodded.

"Nothing is for him. Understood?"

She nodded again.

"You made your own decision to marry Sam, didn't you?"

She gave no answer.

She leered at her.

"I did."

"Right." She smiled. "Every chore is mine today. You need some rest." There was a short pause. "Tomorrow, I'll buy you new clothes."

Nhamo smiled widely.

Mai Pastor got her cellphone and dialed Deaconess Mercy's phone number. Mercy's cellphone rang.

"Hello, Mama?"

"Good morning, Daughter."

"I'm fine. Good morning, Mama."

"Fine. The noisy background is telling me you're at work, right?"

"True."

"Sorry for the disturbance..."

"Don't say that, Mama. It's a blessing to receive a call from you."

"...I want you to tell Sam that he's won the jackpot. But I've to talk to him in person."

"That's really good news for him. I'll tell him to visit you, Mama."

"Thanks. Have a blessed day."

"I receive it, Mama."

Immediately, a smile touched Mai Pastor's lips as she read a phone message from her husband:

Hi, I'm not coming today. Greet my boys and Nhamo.

After reading it, she called Mercy again and told her to contact Sam—she wanted him to come as soon as possible. The marriage proposal had to be discussed during the absence of her husband.

At around 2 p.m., Brother Sam, pushing his bicycle, walked into the yard, a container of fresh milk on the carrier of the bicycle. He positioned the bike under the mango tree, brought down the container and motioned to knock on the door. Before he touched it, he met

Nhamo. "Good morning," he said, his heart pounding.

"Good afternoon, Brother."

He looked down. "I... I... I..."

"Get in."

He shambled in, shamefaced, the container still in his left hand.

Mai Pastor came out of her bedroom; she had made out the visitor's voice.

Sam lifted up his face. "Mama, good afternoon."

"Good afternoon, Sam. Sit down. Nhamo, come. Get the container to the fridge. I'm sure it's ours, right?"

"Yes, it's all for you. When it's finished, feel free to call for some more."

"Thank you. Be blessed."

"I receive the blessing."

"I personally called you here to let you know that Nhamo's accepted your proposal."

Sam smiled widely.

"But there are conditions."

His smile faded and was replaced with anxiety.

"Take care of Nhamo. She left school, when she was in Form Two, because her mother had died. I want her to continue from where she left it. If this is impossible for you, it's better that you leave her alone."

Nhamo was in the kitchen, listening to the conversation, which caused her to build trust in Mai Pastor that she was not betraying her.

Sam looked touched. "I won't hurt her. I promise to take care of her. I'm also an orphan, although I've got a mother. My father died two years ago. He was murdered at a dam called Nyamawanga near Satchel Farm."

"Very sorry, Sam."

"It's ok, Mama."

There was some silence that seemed to be of honoring the death of a hero.

Sam, his eyes turning around, commented to break the silence: "These are beautiful leather sofas."

Mai Pastor smiled. "Thank you."

Nhamo stood by the kitchen door. "Lunch is ready."

"Good girl. Bring it over here." She licked her lips.

After having their lunch, Mai Pastor asked, "How much do you've for *lobola* and the wedding?"

Brother Sam scratched his head and stammered for the first time: "I... I... It d— doesn't tak— take me long to raise it."

"It means you've nothing so far, doesn't it?"

"No. I've something."

Mai Pastor folded her arms and began to muse: *Lobola, according to our custom, is said, accepted and spent by the bride's relatives. Nhamo has no one I know. Who'll do all this?*

Anyway, what's important in life, when you're an orphan, is to find a person who can take care of you. The lobola is not important. So Nhamo must elope to Sam. "When do you want to take her away?"

"Any time. Even today."

She laughed. "Not today. Anyway, what I want first is for Nhamo to go to school. Lobola is a thing to discuss later. What's important is a good marriage with no domestic violence. Is this understood?"

He nodded fast. "Yes."

Nhamo got it all, and she loved it. Now the desire to have a husband bound her; she wished Sam could take her away on that day.

"Prepare to take her home on the first day of January."

"Thank you!" Sam was over the moon.

"But don't tell anyone about this."

He nodded. "I'll keep it as a secret. I won't tell even my mother; I want to surprise her."

Nhamo released a sigh of excitement and thanked God.

CHAPTER 8

O N the first day of January, Sam and Nhamo sneaked from the church, where everyone was praising God for the New Year's Day. They walked in the dark from Glendale Township to Heyshot Farm; that's a distance of about 5km.

At Heyshot, when they reached a fig tree by the road, they turned right and followed a path into the compound. Nhamo was frightened when she heard an owl hoot on the fig tree. It was not one—another flew over them.

"Don't be afraid; they're doves."

"Doves coo"—she whispered—"they don't hoot, and they don't have big heads."

"I know. But owls are harmless. They're just ordinary birds."

She did not answer back.

They went past dorms, walked a while and entered a small yard surrounded with a durawall of grass. Three thatched huts stood inside, their doors almost facing one another. Sam led her into one of them in which he lit a paraffin lamp.

"Sit on the bed, but it's a *sichoka*." He laughed.

"What does that mean?"

He smirked. "It's an immovable bed."

Nhamo did not want to inspect the bed at that moment, but she could feel the mattress was different from those at Mai Pastor's home. Her eyes moved around, studying Sam's possessions: a table with two church books was at the centre, another one with an old radio was in the corner, a clothesline with creased clothes ran across the room, and pictures of gospel musicians and preachers were all over the walls.

"This is Heyshot Farm. You'll see it during the day."

"I heard my mother once worked here."

"Really? I'm sure my mother knew her. I'll ask her. What's her name?"

"Susan Chihera."

"Ok. Mama will tell us."

"I'm thirsty."

"Let me get you some water from the kitchen. Coming soon." He stood up, went outside and brought a mug full of water.

Early in the morning, at around 4 a.m., Sam's mother began to sweep the yard. Two men came pushing a wheelbarrow on which they carried Matumbu. He was too drunk, unable to walk alone. Sam came out and helped his mother carry him into her house.

"Mama"—Sam let the cat out of the bag—"I brought a daughter in-law for you. She's in my room."

"Sam, Sam, Sam." She paused. "How many times have I called you?"

"Three times." He knew his mother was not happy.

"Look at how poor we are. What shall we give her and her family?"

He was dumbfounded.

"You just did it without telling me. Why?"

"I wanted to surprise you."

"And you've succeeded in doing it. I'm surprised for sure. What's next?

"Get out of my sight before I hit you in the face!"

He left and went into his room.

Nhamo looked him in the eyes. "Is anything wrong?"

"Nothing wrong. They just brought my drunk father."

She arced her eyebrows. "Father? Didn't you say your father was murdered?"

"This one's my stepfather."

"Ok."

When the sun rose, Amai Sam spread two sitting mats, one for herself and the other one for her daughter in-law.

"Sam," she called, "Sam."

He ignored her.

Nhamo shook him. "Can't you hear her?"

Sam just got up from the bed, not talking, walked out and stared at his mother, unable to say anything.

"Tell my daughter in-law to feel at home. Let her come out so she can chat with her mother in-law. Her mat is that one."

"Ok, Mama," Sam said smilingly and entered his hut.

Some minutes later, Nhamo followed behind Sam to the mat outside their hut. Amai Sam was attracted by the girl's beauty and humanity.

Sam sat on a stool next to his wife and made brief introductions: "Mama, this is Nhamo, my wife. She's an orphan like me. She says her mother Susan Chihera once worked on this farm."

"Susan Chihera?" She looked astonished. "You're Nhamo, Susan's daughter born within my eyesight?"

Nhamo was openmouthed.

"Your mother was my friend. You're more than a daughter in-law to me; you're my daughter. Feel free. Don't be bound by any traditional custom."

A smile contorted Nhamo's beautiful face.

"When you were a baby, I used to call you my daughter in-law, so it was a prophecy. I—"

Sam interrupted her: "Mama, you're a prophetess. You need to join our church."

She laughed, shrugging. "Let me prepare a welcoming breakfast for my daughter in-law. That big cock must bite the dust today." She got up.

Matumbu coughed and grumbled in Amai Sam's hut: "Where's my tobacco? This practice is really bad. I keep it well, but someone comes to displace it." He patted his pockets and smiled. "Here you are." He tore a piece of paper and made a cigar.

His wife approached him before he stepped out to bask in the morning sun. "Sam's wife is outside."

"My daughter in-law? I can't wait to—"

"Wait." She blocked him. "Your zip is open. You've eye rheum. Clean your eyes first." She closed the zip for him.

After fixing everything, she led him out and directed him to sit on the mortar bench of her hut. Before Nhamo and Matumbu greeted each other, she formally made some introductions: "My daughter in-law, this is your father in-law.

"Baba Sam, this is Sam's wife, your daughter in-law. Guess what? She's Nhamo, Susan Chihera's daughter, from your village."

Nhamo and Matumbu were stunned when they recognised each other. Nhamo had changed a little; now, clad in beautiful clothes, she looked smart and more gorgeous. Her head was covered with a multi-colored doek, and a wrapper similar to the doek covered the bottom of her body.

"I thought you're in Harare with Charles Soko and his wife. What happened?" Matumbu gaped.

"We shifted from Harare last month."

"Do they know you've eloped with a farm boy?"

Nhamo drooped her head.

Sam and his mother drooped theirs, too.

There was a wave of silence.

CHAPTER 9

A T the church, everyone was celebrating the New Year's Day. They sang, danced, prayed and chatted. Nhamo and Sam were nowhere to be found.

"Mai," Pastor asked, seated in his office.

"Baba," Mai Pastor replied.

"Why've you sent Nhamo home, while her friends are celebrating this great day?"

"She's gone to check the house."

Deaconess Mercy, serving them with breakfast, hid a smirk on her face by turning aside.

"It's ok." Pastor nodded. "But she must come back to join the others."

"I'm sure she's fallen asleep," Mai said.

Mercy washed Mai Pastor's hands and walked out of the office. As soon as she closed the door behind her, she began to laugh alone. "Is this a holy lie from a woman who serves God?

"Anyway..." She dismissed it all with a shrug.

At around 10 a.m., Matumbu was at Glendale Musika Rank, a designated place where buses officially ranked to pick up or drop off their passengers. When he saw a light-blue bus with dark-blue horizontal lines, he smiled, but a board displayed behind the left window screen of the bus read CHIWESHE in capital letters. Matumbu scowled when he read it; he wanted the one that read MUKUMBURA.

Another bus came. It was yellow with green horizontal lines. Its board read MKUMBURA—it did not have a U after M. That confused him, and the bus was new to him. He motioned and asked the driver, "Are you going to Mukumbura? I'm Matumbu; I live in Chiutsi Village. I'm—"

"See the conductor, dude."

"Not Jude, but Matumbu." He hurried to the passengers' door, holding a 5ltr container full of homemade beer. He wore a black creased t-shirt and brown creased trousers. His feet were partially covered with torn shoes.

On the bus, he sat next to a stout woman, who made him sit with one buttock.

The bus left Glendale. Matumbu was in high spirits that in five hours he would be delivering the latest gospel to the people of his village. However, the journey was not that pleasant; the stout lady, with her elbow, was digging him into the ribs.

"What's your destination?" he asked, looking at the woman's fat face.

"Mukumbura Border, after your place. I've to reach Mozambique today." She had a husky voice.

"Grr!" Matumbu looked aside. He wanted so much to change the position, but the bus was full, and some people were standing in the passageway.

The lady farted loud and accused him of having done it. Those who had heard the fart laughed, but the other ones complained.

At around 3 p.m., the bus stopped at Munanga Bus Stop. Matumbu disembarked, stretched himself and crossed the road to the other side. Some villagers laughed at him as they saw him walking with no groceries, but just a 5ltr container of beer from which he drank a moment before he walked to a desolate home of the late Granny Chihera.

He stood in front of Granny's hut, whose roof had already collapsed inside, and knocked on the door, shouting, "Open this door, Granny Chihera! I've a story to tell you! I know you won't like it!

"I know you're dead, but I believe your spirit lives in this hut!" He paused and drank from his container.

A number of onlookers had already surrounded him, wondering if he had gone mad. His wife and his two daughters were crying. Baba Soko and Mai Soko, Pastor's parents, gaped at him as he performed.

He continued: "I'm not mad! I'm drinking, but I'm not drunk! I know what I'm doing and saying, my people!

"This is evil! How can a pastor and his wife take away an orphan and give her to a farm boy to marry? Pastor Charles Soko and his wife are evil! They failed to look after Nhamo! Today, they have betrayed her!" He paused and drank. "I wasn't supposed to travel this day, but I failed to keep this news! I respect you, my people! Thank you!" He proceeded to his home, his family following behind him.

Frustrated, Baba Soko snatched a cellphone from his own pocket and phoned his son: "Tell me! What the hell is going on there?"

"What's wrong, Baba?" Pastor asked, confused.

"Where's Nhamo?"

"At home."

"Whose home?"

"Mine."

"Right now, Matumbu is telling the whole village that Nhamo is married. What does this mean?"

Pastor's mind was disturbed. He threw his Bible onto the table and pushed the office door to close. It dawned on him that Sam was not around—that was unusual. The boy loved to stand behind the pulpit most of the time, so his absence was easily noticed.

Mai Pastor called, knocking on the door, "Daddy, open the door!"

He got up and shambled to it. "Get in." He closed it again.

"People have queued outside to get in for counselling. Why've you closed the door?" She sat down, anxiously waiting for an answer.

"Are you my helper or my destroyer?"

"What question is that?"

"Where's Nhamo?"

"She's at home."

"What do you really take me for? A fool?"

She remained silent, and her heart was pounding.

"Where's Sam?"

"How do I know?"

"Don't make me sin against my God. These are the ten days of January prayers, and you've started my first day with a temptation."

"I don't know what you're talking about."

He frowned at her. "Don't you? Just now, my father has phoned me. Matumbu is telling the whole village that Nhamo is married."

Matumbu, she thought, *knows it. How?* "How? Who told him this wrong information?"

"I'm really staying with a she-devil. I need Nhamo back." He lost control and slapped her.

She fell onto the floor. "I'm sorry." She was sobbing.

Pastor left the office, angry. As he was walking away—outside the church premise—he met a madman in rags, who asked him, "Why are you angry on this New Year's Day when you're supposed to be praising with your friends? Did your pastor send you away from others? Are you a prodigal son? Go back to your Father. Anger doesn't solve anything. Don't create a problem to solve another problem. Don't try to attach a fallen fruit back to its mother tree. Let bygones be bygones. Open a new page and write a new chapter."

Pastor's cellphone rang. He just looked at it, unable to answer it.

"Answer it!" the madman commanded.

"Hello, Daddy!"

"Don't let this incident eat you up. Just wait for me; I'll come there after the days of your prayers."

"Thank you." He slid his cellphone into one of his jacket pockets and stared at the madman now disappearing into an unfinished church building next to theirs. Stunned, he walked back to his office, asked his wife to forgive him for the slap and helped the people who needed counselling.

Two days after the prayers, on Saturday, Baba Soko was at Westview in Glendale Township, chatting with his grandsons, eating some fruits.

On Monday, they were at Amai Sam's home.

"I'm happy you've come in peace," Amai Sam said. "This means God is in it."

Baba Soko nodded; meanwhile, Pastor drooped his head.

"Nhamo was left in our care," Baba Soko explained. "I take her as my granddaughter. She's an orphan, but not alone. We're her relatives; for any challenge, contact us."

"She's my only daughter in-law, the wife of my only son. I'm obliged to take care of her. Don't be afraid."

Nhamo smiled widely, seated on a mat next to Sam's stool.

"As her husband, I promise not to abuse her."

"This is all good"—Baba Soko added—"but, Nhamo, be a good person, too. Take care of your husband and your mother in-law. Do good things for others if you want them to do good things for you."

She agreed with a nod.

Pastor, at last, nodded and said, "Let your marriage be blessed. Don't give up coming to church, both of you. Whenever you need help, feel free to approach me."

"Thank you," they said simultaneously, broad smiles on their faces.

"You're welcome."

CHAPTER 10

ONE day, an unfriendly weather caused Matumbu to wear three jerseys. He sat on a stool by the fire in the kitchen, turning his stale *sadza* over so that each side of it could receive enough heat to roast well. At the same time, he was roasting a large piece of goat meat.

Amai Sam was also by the fire, warming herself. She looked unhappy. "You ran away with your friends' money. They came here complaining until I paid them with my own 20 dollars; I need it back."

"You've been saying this since yesterday. Didn't I tell you that I'll repay it?" Matumbu complained. "From where do you think I can get it fast? Do you want me to steal? From whose bank?"

"That's being rude!" she scowled. "You need to be grateful! The day you left this home, you didn't tell anyone. I was shocked to see your friends approach me complaining that they had sent you away with a 5ltr container to buy some beer for them. It's reported that you bought the beer, received the change and travelled to your rural. You did that without their consent. They wanted to report you to the police, but I calmed them down and refunded the money."

"Why did you stop them? You think I fear the police?"

She frowned. "Don't you make me angry. From the first day of January up to this day, the fifteenth of July, how many days, weeks or months are there? You've been afraid of coming back."

"I haven't been afraid of anything; all along, I've been with my family at my rural home. I've a village; I can't be compared with farm fools."

"Don't mention your rural family to me; it makes me vomit! Why have you come back then? Who called you back? Why can't you just live with your rural family without bothering us, the farm fools?"

"Fine, let's call it a day. I'll pay you the money. Don't spoil my breakfast." He took away his roasted breakfast and began to eat.

Sam and his wife were in their room, covered with blankets.

Sam asked, caressing Nhamo's stomach, "Yesterday, you refused to eat the goat meat brought by your father in-law. Why? Is it because of this new pregnancy of yours?"

"No," she said softly and lovely, "that's not the matter. It's because I know Matumbu better than you. Apart from being my father in-law, he's my *sahwira*; he buried my mother and my grandmother.

"At his rural home, he owns no goats, even a single chicken. He steals and kills stray goats from other villages."

"Really?"

"Yes, but don't betray me."

"I won't, but I'll find a way to let Mama know this. The way won't jeopardize you, I promise you."

Back in the kitchen, Matumbu had changed the subject and was now blaming Amai Sam for welcoming Nhamo into their family.

"That's none of your business. It's my son's choice," Amai Sam retorted to what Matumbu had just said.

"It's none of my business, right?" Matumbu spoke with the food in his mouth. "I speak like a madman, but what I say is always found working in the future.

"How can he marry a girl whose relatives don't exist? To whom is he going to give the bride price for her? Consider this; it's a serious issue.

"Something surprising is that your son is sending her to school. This is abomination. Wives aren't sent to school; they abandon their husbands when they're educated."

"You're a dinosaur. You've got old beliefs that don't apply to this modern life. You're too primitive. Let Nhamo go to school; she'll help her husband."

"One day, you'll remember my words."

"I won't remember foolish words."

"You don't understand it because you're a woman, too. I'll rather talk to Sam... Never send a wife to school. Period."

"Don't mislead my son, please."

He finished his food and licked his fingers until they became clean, as if he had used water to wash them. He reached for a mug full of water and gulped from it. Patting on his stomach, he nodded, a weak smile trying to tear his lips. "Where're your gumboots?"

"What for?"

"I want to visit Mhararano Canteen to meet my friends from Chimugan'a Farm. They want to buy me some beer."

"Everyone's in their house because of this cold weather. What's so special about beer?"

"You don't want to give me your gumboots, do you?"

"Take them from the bedroom." She paused a moment. "But when you think of disappearing to your village again, don't go with my gumboots; I'm warning you."

He went out of the kitchen and walked to the bedroom. After putting the gumboots on, he paid attention to make out his wife's footsteps if she was following him. Then, he pulled out a large piece of goat meat from a sack, wrapped it with a small plastic bag and hid it inside his pant. He sneaked out of the room and then out of the yard.

"Auntie Rose," Matumbu said to a bar lady standing behind a buffet, the wrapped meat now in his left palm, "I've brought you a large piece of goat meat going only for a small price equivalent to a litre of opaque beer."

"I've to see the meat first."

"That's not a problem." Matumbu looked around first and then placed it onto the counter.

The bar lady unwrapped it and licked her lips. "I need it." She looked at him. "Do you need cash or beer?"

"Beer."

She walked to the shelves and brought one litre of opaque beer for him.

He took it and went to occupy a chair in one of the corners. He was the only one drinking in the premise. Some minutes later, three men joined him. Matumbu bought some more beer, but on credit—he would pay Auntie Rose with meat.

In the evening, when Matumbu was home, chatting with his wife, a boy came and said,

"Auntie Rose sent me to collect some goat meat from you."

"What're you talking about?" He pretended not to know anything.

His wife emphasised: "Auntie Rose needs the goat meat you promised her. I don't know on what grounds!"

"Lad, go and tell her to mind her tongue!" He sent the boy away.

Embarrassed, the boy shambled away and began to run when he was outside the yard. He carried the message as it was to Auntie Rose, who quickly closed the doors of the bar and hit the road to Amai Sam's homestead, where her target stayed. She reached the home and stood akimbo in front of Matumbu.

He welcomed her with a provoking question: "What do you want from me, woman?"

"You're lucky"—she said, pointing her shaking finger at him—"I respect your wife. Had she not been present, I'd have kicked your balls!"

Amai Sam calmed her: "Take it easy, Auntie Rose. What happened?"

"He borrowed beer from my bar and promised to pay me with meat," she explained.

Matumbu laughed. "Beer on credit? The police and the law in our country don't allow anyone to sell liquor on credit. What the hell are you talking about?"

"You hear him?" Auntie blew her fuse.

"Please, calm down, Auntie. Leave everything to me," his wife begged. "I'm giving you the meat."

"No longer interested! Keep it! And don't worry about the wasted beer! I'll see what I can do about it! Goodbye!" She stormed out of the yard.

"Go! I don't care about your plot against me! I'm Matumbu 'Special'. Wizards and witches once tried to harm me, but they failed!" he shouted, a wry of I don't care contorting his drunk-looking face.

CHAPTER 11

ONE night, Sam and his fellow irrigators Hwanda, Jimmy and Mabvuto sat by a big fire, sharing true and false stories.

"Although this fire is big," Sam said, trying to push a big log into the fire, "it's taking too long to dry our drenched overalls."

"The log needs two people." Mabvuto got up and helped him.

"This big fire"—Hwanda laughed—"reminds me of Jeke's story. Do you all know Jeke?"

"That driver of an FM tractor, the former irrigator," Mabvuto said, "who left his friends warming themselves by a big fire like this and went away to defecate behind a big bush. When he came back, he began to complain that his friends were farting and stinking, not knowing he had a piece of his own poop stuck on the collar of his overall."

"Yes, that one. Haha." Hwanda laughed. "He would have died in a nightmare had his workmate not woken him up.

"Their fire was big like this. His gumboot caught the fire, when he was asleep, and began to burn reeking of some unpleasant smell. When it was happening, he was dreaming about a war in which enemies had thrown a bomb whose gases were stinking like a burning rubber. He didn't know it was his gumboot burning and stinking until his workmate woke him up."

They laughed.

Sam joked: "Whoever promoted him to be a driver saved his life from irrigators' fire."

"I heard that John"—Hwanda changed the subject—"allowed his workers to invite a witchdoctor into this farm to solve issues of abnormal miscarriages with women. Is it true?"

Jimmy leered at him, not talking.

"So I heard," Mabvuto said.

"Let it be so," Sam said. "A week ago, my wife incurred this miscarriage problem. At the same night, two other women whose names I can't disclose also faced the same."

Sam's friends empathized with him, except Jimmy.

Sam continued: "Our farm needs to be spiritually cleansed. There're too many witches and wizards. If this witchdoctor comes, things will be better."

"It's ten minutes before eleven o'clock now," Mabvuto said after glancing at his wristwatch. "Let's go change the position of the irrigation pipes."

Unwillingly, they left the fire.

After thirty minutes, they came back to the fire, convulsing with the cold.

A security guard patrolling around the wheat field approached them and warmed himself by the fire, too. "Is this Sam?"

Sam lifted up his face. "Yes."

"What's wrong with you, young man?" the security guard asked.

"Wrong?" Sam was surprised.

"I heard that you're sending your wife to school."

Jimmy chipped in: "Yes, he's sending her. He needs some advice. He's playing with naked fire."

Sam sneered. "So, Jimmy, you've been reserving your strength in order to use it to speak nonsense against my decisions and my plans?"

"I'm trying to help you," Jimmy said. "I witnessed many men being abandoned by their wives after they sent them to school."

"You're right, dude." The security guard seconded Jimmy.

"Don't compare them with me and my wife. My wife has true love for me. She's a God-given helper. Our marriage is blessed."

"One day," the security guard said, "you'll remember my words."

"Mister, leave us right now before I hit you with this piece of firewood!" Sam warned the security guard. "Jealous wizards! Sons of witches! A witchdoctor is coming soon to disgrace you!"

The security guard walked away sheepishly.

Jimmy kept quiet.

Mabvuto and Hwanda remained silent as they were, not commenting.

A month later, the farm residents gathered on a soccer ground for Tsikamutanda, the witchdoctor. Each of them was instructed to cross a decorated rod laid on the ground. Those who were clean in spirit crossed it without any difficulty, and they were sent out of the soccer ground. The unclean ones found it difficult to cross the rod; they felt dizzy and collapsed.

When the unclean were left alone at the centre of the soccer field, each of them had their secrets disclosed by the witchdoctor. Among them were Matumbu and Jimmy.

"This young man," Tsikamutanda shouted to the top of his voice, "has a male goblin that causes miscarriages to the women it sleeps with! By saying *it sleeps with*, I mean *it has sexual intercourse with*!

"Young man, drink this water from my calabash!"

Jimmy drank Tsikamutanda's water.

"Now, go and bring your goblin here!"

He sprinted away.

"You." Tsikamutanda pointed at Matumbu. "Your hands are dripping with innocent blood of more than one person!

"You've a male lightning making your two mature daughters wives! Because of it, your daughters are not married!

"One night, you tried to use the lightning to strike an innocent woman, but it failed to work! Hence, you stood up by yourself and went to her home, where you lit and burnt her two houses! She was burnt inside! You've to confess to her daughter!" The witchdoctor paused and chanted for a moment. "Right now, call her daughter to come in!"

"Nhamo!" Matumbu called.

Nhamo walked in, surprised.

"I killed your mother"—he confessed—"I was afraid she would disclose to my first wife that I had married a second wife. I personally burnt her house, during the night, after my magic lightning had refused to strike her."

Nhamo wept, and Sam took her away from the soccer field.

Tsikamutanda continued: "Drink from this calabash! Don't use your lightning again! The day you try to use it is the day you'll die! This is the reason you're drinking from this calabash! This is *muteyo*, a snare to trap you!"

Tsikamutanda motioned and touched the left shoulder of a very old woman next to Matumbu. "During the day, she's a very weak old woman! But during the night, she's an energetic girl!

"She visits men and has sexual intercourse with them during the night! Many of you slept with her!

"Drink my water! This is *muteyo*! Don't do it again! You'll die!"

She drank it.

Jimmy brought his goblin. It had a protruding manhood, and it looked like a carved doll. Its waist had beads.

Tsikamutanda's men made a big fire and burnt the goblin and other witchcraft items.

The very day, Amai Sam divorced Matumbu and chased him away from her home.

CHAPTER 12

SOMETIME in October, there was joy at Amai Sam's home. Nhamo was over the moon for passing her school exams. Amai Sam danced and ululated. Sam whistled and danced too. Their neighbours peeped through the holes in the thatched durawall.

"I thank you, Mama." Nhamo curtsied in front of her mother in-law. "I was married at the age of 14, but now I'm 18. You're taking good care of me. No complaint. Be blessed."

"You're more than a daughter in-law to me, I told you."

"But"—Nhamo's face fell—"something is always eating me up. I don't have a baby for your son. I—"

"Don't worry yourself, my daughter." She hugged her. "A child is a gift from God. He'll give you when time comes. Always, learn to wait for God's time."

"It's true, my love." Sam patted her. "With or without a child, I love you."

She smiled at her husband.

Amai Sam left the two and went to Mhararano Shop, where she borrowed 2kg of rice, 750ml of cooking oil, 500g of salt and 250g of *Matemba*. Whoever she met, she proudly told them about her daughter in-law. On her way home, she borrowed a live chicken from a certain woman.

"Welcome back, Mama." Nhamo walked to meet her. "Let me help you."

"Thank you." She handed her the chicken and carried the remainder. "You can slaughter it. That's for our lunch. If some is left, it's for our supper."

Nhamo slaughtered and dressed it. After that, she cooked for the family.

The day was a bit hot in the afternoon, so— after taking their lunch—they spread their mats under a peach tree and chatted. Sam and Nhamo sat on theirs, and Amai Sam was on hers. A mug of water was beside them.

"Help me choose a career." Nhamo looked at Sam and then at her mother in-law.

"Career?" Sam and his mother looked at each other, surprised.

"Yes."

"What's that?" asked Sam.

Nhamo smirked. "It's a professional job; for example, teaching and nursing."

Amai Sam stared at Sam for a moment.

Sam shrugged. "I've no idea about how people become teachers and nurses. I only know how John employs his farm workers."

"I also have no idea," said Nhamo's mother in-law.

Nhamo understood them.

"Just be what you want to be. Follow your heart's desire," Sam said.

Nhamo mused, *I can apply to join the police. My schoolmate knows the procedure. Her uncle is a policeman. Besides that, she always wanted to be a police officer. The two of us can encourage each other.* "I think I can join the police."

"You want to be a policeman?" Amai Sam asked, startled.

"A policewoman, not a policeman," Sam said, laughing.

"Don't laugh at Mama." Nhamo leered at him and then looked at her mother in-law. "Yes, Mama, I want to be a police officer. My friend, who resides at Sisk in Glendale, will help me join it. Her uncle is a policeman. She also wants to join it."

"Ok." She paused for a moment, musing. "Will you be still friendly, my daughter? It looks as if many of them are not friendly."

"I won't change, Mama. You're my family. How can I do that? I'm here to help you."

Sam smiled. *I got this one from God; she won't do that.*

"When do you want to go?" Amai Sam asked, worried.

"Tomorrow, I'll visit Glendale Police Station to enquire."

"Ok, my in-law."

The following day, Nhamo woke up very early in the morning and carried out all her chores. When Sam and his mother woke up, she had already prepared breakfast for them and some *maheu* to drink at work.

The time the farm workers left the compound for work was the time Nhamo left for Glendale Police Station. Unfortunately, when she reached the station, the office she was referred to was still closed. So she had to wait until 8 a.m.

At 7.40 a.m., she saw Sergeant Zhira walk straight to the cabin office and unlocked its door. She followed him and knocked on the door.

"Come in." He was piling papers on his table. "What can I do for you?"

"I want to be a policewoman."

He stared at her a moment and asked, "Did you pass English, Science and Mathematics?"

"I did."

"Are they five subjects in all?"

"Yes."

"How many sittings?"

"One."

"Ok. Come back after 30 minutes." He walked from the table to the door. "Wait for me outside."

Nhamo stepped out.

Some minutes later, two boys and three girls joined her. They wanted to apply for the job, too.

After 20 minutes, a young policewoman came and opened the door. Later, Sergeant Zhira came and called Nhamo to get in.

"What's your name?" he asked.

"Nhamo."

The female police officer stopped typing and leered at her. "You want him to ask for your surname separately?"

"Chihera. Nhamo Chihera," she said, shamefaced.

"This organisation is looking forward to employing clever people, not fools." She continued on her typewriter.

"Give me your national ID, your birth certificate and your results," Sergeant said, stretching out his right hand towards her.

She handed them over to him.

"I see." The sergeant nodded. "Have them photocopied and bring the photocopies."

"Ok." Nhamo stood up and left the office. Now, her worry was about where she could get the money to photocopy the documents. She did not want to bother Mai Pastor at her home in Westview. Finally, she went back and presented her challenge to the officers.

"You say you don't have money?" The policewoman laughed. "Then go home."

Nhamo hesitated to leave the office.

The policewoman frowned. "Don't waste—"

"Take this." Sergeant Zhira handed her four coins. "Hurry. I need to process your papers."

"Thank you, sir." She bowed down before leaving.

After ten minutes, she came back with the copies and was given forms to fill in.

"I expect you to bring these forms within four workdays," Sergeant said.

"Thank you, sir."

The female police officer laughed and said, "You're full of too much respect, lady."

"She's right"—Sergeant praised her—"Keep it up. I wish you were my daughter."

"Maybe she is yours, Serge."

"You want to pick on me now," he said, laughing.

CHAPTER 13

AT a police training depot in Harare, Nhamo deliberated on quitting the training. Her two friends had quit the previous day. If it was not of her poor life background, she would have gone with them.

I'm in a tough situation, she thought. *It's now a week, but it seems as if I've been here for a month or so... I miss Sam and Mama.*

Suddenly, her squad instructor, a slim woman with big probing eyes, entered the barrack and stood at the door near the senior recruit's bed. Nhamo's stomach churned and groaned as she saw her.

"You allowed two recruits to quit yesterday, right?" she asked the senior recruit in charge of the others.

"No, Ma—"

"Don't answer back!" She landed her slap on her cheek, and it thundered.

The junior recruits' faces fell.

"I see you're sympathizing with her, right?

"Everyone, get out and fetch some water! Move! Move! You're too slow!" She began to slap them one by one as they ran out through the door.

Buckets of water on their shaved heads, the recruits walked back into the barrack. The instructor commanded them to pour the water onto the floor and then ordered them to mop it.

"Unless you finish mopping, you won't sleep tonight!" She walked out slowly, saying, "This whole week, I'm with you! I want to fix you!"

Nhamo leered at her. *Evil woman. For how long are you going to ill-treat us? 6 months? 7 months?*

If I had a stable family, I wouldn't be doing this.

They worked; meanwhile, they were dozing. At around 2 a.m., the barrack was clean, and they went to bed. At exactly 3 a.m., they heard male recruits shout for everyone to come out for accountability. They woke up unwillingly and ran to a parade ground. The instructor was already there waiting for them.

Each squad sat in a single file. Nhamo's was the last of all the squads, and its members were the last to be counted.

"Who's clapped there?" The instructor charged towards Nhamo's squad. "Who has clapped hands?"

No one answered her.

"You don't want to tell me, eh? Get down and roll!"

"It's Chihera." A faint-hearted recruit exposed her.

"Chihera, bring yourself here!"

Nhamo got up and walked to her.

She brought her face close to Nhamo's. "What was that for?"

"I was trying to kill a mosquito." Her voice was trembling.

"Why?"

"It was sucking my blood."

"Just that?"

"Yes."

"If it doesn't suck your blood, from where do you think it will get its food?"

Nhamo did not answer her.

"Have you ever seen it farming or buying food from the market?" She made two short steps backwards.

"I—"

She slapped her and kicked her.

Nhamo staggered to her squad, tears forming in her eyes.

"No one is going to sleep. Stay here until 5 a.m., the time we want to start our morning run.

"You don't just sit; sing!"

This is the wrong end of the stick, Nhamo thought and joined her mates in a boring song, which they sang till 5 a.m.

From the parade ground, they jogged up and down the streets, singing motivational songs. They did it for an hour. After it, they bathed, breakfasted and waited for the programs of the day.

Two months later, Nhamo became accustomed to every situation in the police training depot. When they were released for the first time on a payday, she went to town, bought new clothes and kept them in her barrack locker. The next payday, she visited her husband and her mother in-law.

Sam and his mother were on a mat under the peach tree, eating *sadza* with pumpkin leaves, when Nhamo entered the yard, carrying a small bag on her back and a large one on her head. Having noticed her, the two sprang up and ran to her, jumping up with joy like calves springing up in front of their mothers. Amai Sam took down the large bag; Sam carried the small one.

"Get in, my in-law," she called from the kitchen, positioning the bags.

"No, Mama. I need some fresh air here. Under this peach tree." She sat down on the mat. "Sam, come, my hubby. Long time."

"Long time." He walked fast from the kitchen, holding a mug of water.

Nhamo received the mug with two hands and gulped from it. "Thanks for the water, Daddy."

"Do you need some more?"

"No."

"Is this the end of the training?" he asked, sitting down near her.

"No, I'm just here for about three or four hours. By exactly 6 p.m., I must be at the depot."

Sam looked worried.

"Don't worry, I'll be visiting you like this."

He smiled.

Sam's mother was standing near them, smiling. "How're you, my in-law?"

"Great, Mama. I've got a short time with you. Can you bring the bags here; I want to show you the things I bought for you. Sorry, I'm sending you, Mama."

"Don't worry, my lovely daughter in-law," she said and walked to the kitchen.

Sam got up to help her.

As Nhamo gave them the clothes and the groceries, their shouts of joy filled the yard and crossed over to their neighbours, who came and peeped through the holes in the thatched durawall.

"Thank you, my in-law." She stood up, ululating, and danced.

Sam got up, too, and joined the dance.

Some of the neighbours came to see Nhamo. They asked her to help their children join the police. Some began to report cases to her. Within herself, she laughed and said: *I'm still a recruit; I can't help your children. I can't solve your cases.*

Sam and his mother wore some of their new clothes, which fitted them. In front of the onlookers, they walked proudly, praising Nhamo.

One of the onlookers shouted, "Those who were saying, 'Don't send your wife to school,' are now embarrassed!"

Jimmy was among them, and it did not go well with him. Embarrassed, he sneaked away. Hwanda and Mabvuto, Sam's workmates, came to congratulate Sam's wife. There was much joy.

At around 3 p.m., Nhamo left the compound. Everyone was left with her name on their lips. Everywhere, the story was hers.

"Look at this"—Amai Sam shed tears of joy—"I praise you, God. Since I was born, this is my first time in life to wear a suit and new leather shoes I call my own."

"Even this food, Mama," said Sam. "Look at the tinned foods. This grocery will take us up to two months."

"Your wife is from God, Sam."

"That's true, Mama."

During the night, the family did not sleep well. Two owls were hooting on the peach tree. That had never happened before. Sam prayed fervently in his room. His mother cringed in hers, her body fully covered with blankets.

After praying, he got outside, and the owls flapped away.

CHAPTER 14

AFTER the training, Nhamo was deployed to work in Masvingo Province.

"Welcome to Masvingo Province," a male senior police officer in charge of Masvingo Police Province—with a broad smile on his face—said to the new junior police officers seated in a conference room. "This is not a police training depot. You're no longer police recruits. Now you're qualified police officers, who have successfully accomplished their training. Let bygones be bygones. Don't have grudges on those instructors, who trained you. Whatever they did to you was part of training."

Nhamo scratched her head. *Including slapping me for trying to kill that little bloodsucker? Was it part of training to let the mosquito feed on my blood?*

The senior police officer continued: "At training depots, instructors make you do a lot of things you don't understand, which look stupid or weird. They do it for your advantage."

Has he read my mind? Nhamo scratched her head again.

"I'm giving you ten days of time off so that you can visit your families and tell them about your new stations. Some might think you're still at the training depots." He laughed. "So they need to know you are now out for good.

"Before you go home, the police officers in charge of manpower distribution will give you the police stations to which you'll report after your time off.

"I'm a man of few words, so I'm done with you."

A sergeant guiding the new police officers stood up and brought himself to an attention position. "Junior police officers, attention!"

They rose to his command.

He saluted. "Thank you, sir."

The senior police officer—while seated—pushed his hands forward and brought them back.

The sergeant led his juniors out of the conference room, and they walked downstairs to his office.

Nhamo asked, "How long is it from Masvingo to Harare?"

"About 300km," Sergeant replied, unlocking his office. "Do you come from Harare?"

"No. I come from Glendale, a township outside Harare. Not too far from it, though."

"Umm, that's a long distance from here," he commiserated.

They sat down in the office.

"Luckily, you've all been recommended to work in this town under Masvingo Central Police Station."

They all smiled, looking at one another.

"Don't forget the date of reporting for work at this station."

"We won't," they answered in unison.

After some minutes, they were dismissed.

The following day, Nhamo bussed from Masvingo to Harare. From Harare to Glendale, a certain businessman carried her in his car.

When she was dropped off in Glendale, she got a lift to Heyshot Farm. People admired her in a police uniform.

"That's Sam's wife," one of the people said.

"This is really good. I'll send my wife to school," one young man said.

"Me too," another said.

An old man among them commented: "Not every apple is a good apple. Some of you. Your wives can't even spell out their names. Don't think such dogs can learn new tricks."

Everyone laughed.

As Nhamo approached home, she was touched to see Sam shedding tears; he was on the mortar bench of his mother's hut. She walked fast and squatted beside him. "What's wrong, Sam?" She looked him in the eyes. "Where's Mama?"

"She's too sick."

Nhamo entered her mother in-law's room. "Mama, where are you?" She closed and reopened her eyes for them to be accustomed to the darkness.

"Welcome, my in-law," she spoke from her mat and coughed.

The cough did not sound well as it got into Nhamo's ears. It was similar to the one Granny Chihera coughed before she breathed her last. Tears welled up in her eyes. "What's wrong, Mama?"

"Fever." Her voice was low.

Nhamo touched her with the back of her hand and felt that her head was too hot. "Sam, go and hire a car; I'll pay them any amount."

"No," she objected. "Let Sam come in."

Nhamo called, "Come in, Sam!"

He got in and sat on the floor.

She coughed again. "Take care of each other. Life is full of temptations and challenges. Help each other."

Sam's heart pounded. "What's the meaning of that, Mama?"

That's how Granny Chihera died, Nhamo thought, sobbing. "Mama, don't leave us alone."

She coughed hard and, all of a sudden, became silent.

Nhamo checked her pulses—there was no action. "She's dead."

Sam sprang up and wept, his right hand on his head. The neighbours heard the weep and hurried up to find out what the matter was. It was a disaster. They were shocked because—two days ago—Amai Sam was healthy. They had not heard anything about her health complications.

The news spread. Many people gathered.

A certain woman commented: "They bewitched her because of her daughter in-law's prosperity."

"That's true," another woman agreed. "We need Tsikamutanda to clean the mess again. It's been a long time since we called him. Five years have gone by now."

Pastor and Mai Pastor were informed. They came with the members of their church.

Amai Sam was buried at Nyamawanga Graveyard, where her husband was laid to rest.

A week later, Hwanda and Mabvuto were at work, lining up their irrigation pipes.

"Mabvuto," Hwanda asked, "did you see how Sam's wife sponsored that funeral?"

"Yes, she bought everything."

"It's good to send a wife to school. Look at it; Sam is no longer a farm irrigator. He's now with his wife in Masvingo City, doing better things."

"It's good, but you can't send a wife like mine to school," Mabvuto said, laughing. "She can't even write her name correctly. Instead of Catherine, she writes Katarina."

Laughing, Hwanda intentionally dropped an irrigation pipe and began to clap his hands. "What about her birth certificate? Which name is on it? Maybe it's Katarina, not Catherine."

"I checked it; it's Catherine, not Katarina."

Hwanda picked up the pipe, still laughing. "It's funny."

At Westview, Pastor and Mai Pastor were in their house. Their boys had gone to school.

"Thank you for the breakfast," Pastor said.

"You're welcome, Daddy."

"Nhamo is now a changed person, Mai Pastor."

"That's true. Her life is the work of God. God exalts those who're despised."

"In this one, God used you for her breakthrough. She was married to Sam because of you. Thank you."

She smiled.

A cellphone rang. Pastor picked it up. It was his father calling him from the rural.

Mai Pastor asked after the phone conversation, "Who's that?"

"It's Baba telling me shocking news."

"What news?" She paid attention.

"Matumbu is going mad right now. He's blurting out that he murdered a man at Heyshot Farm and took over his wife."

"Really?" Her eyebrows formed arcs. "He was married to Sam's mother, whose husband was murdered at a dam called Nyamawaka."

"I know the dam; it's Nyamawanga, not Nyamawaka."

"I think he's the one who murdered him. I'll find out."

"From where? Are you a police detective?" Pastor laughed.

"This does not need a police detective. It's clear. Matumbu murdered Sam's father and took over his wife," she said boldly, stood up and walked to the kitchen.

CHAPTER 15

NEAR Masvingo Central Police Station, a speeding taxi screeched to a stop in front of red traffic robots. It had almost hit the back of a private car stopped in front of it.

Nhamo complained from the back seat: "What's wrong with you, Mr Driver? Can't you see the robot is red?"

"I'm sorry, guys."

"I've hired you to drive us safely around Masvingo showing us the town and the locations, not to kill us in an accident, right?"

"Sure. I'm sorry."

"He's apologizing." Sam patted Nhamo on her thigh.

"Ok. Let's go; the robot is now green," she said.

"Thank you." He drove. *How can I concentrate on driving, while you're romancing behind me?*

"Drive us to a food outlet you know," Nhamo said, caressing Sam's thighs.

The driver saw them in a view mirror in the car. "Ok, Madam. Is Chicken Inn ok for you?"

"It's ok."

But stop romancing. You are confusing me here.

The taxi parked at Chicken Inn opposite The High Court of Zimbabwe. The young couple got down. The taxi driver stared at Nhamo's back and at her legs as she walked away. As they came back, small boxes and cans of drinks in their hands, he shifted his eyes to look at the lady's face, at her breast and at the area of her womanhood.

They got in. "Now, take us to the locations," she said.

"Ok, Madam." He looked in the view mirror.

"The logistic to take us around the locations depends on your choice because you're the one who knows the places," she said.

"In each location, I'm going to show you the business centre only."

She nodded. "Sounds good."

Sam nodded, too.

"You can tell us in brief so that we know at least something about the tour," she said.

"Well. From here, I'm taking you to Rujeko A, B and C. From there, I'll take you to Pangolin, Majange, Yeukai, Gomba and Sisk, where you reside. These are the main places to know first. As time goes on, you'll know the other ones.

"We've low density suburbs: Rhodene, Eastview, and so on. These are in the opposite direction."

"Ok, let's go," she said, chewing a piece of chicken.

They left the town.

At the end of the tour, they were dropped off at their home.

"Madam, can I have your cellphone number? I like to keep my clients' contact details." The driver held his cellphone.

"No problem." She gave him the number. "I also need yours. This will help us when we need transport."

Sam nodded.

He gave it to her.

Nhamo's cellphone rang as she opened the door to her room. It was Mai Pastor calling her. She answered and turned on a loud speaker for Sam also to hear the conversation. They sat on their bed.

"Hello, Mama?"

"Hello. How're you?"

"Very fine. And you?"

"Great. I've shocking news."

"Shocking news?" She looked at Sam.

"Yes. Matumbu has committed suicide this afternoon."

"Shame. Why?"

"He became mentally challenged in the morning and began to blurt out that he murdered a man at Heyshot Farm and took over his wife."

"Sure? This is really shocking."

"Sure. I think he's the one who killed Sam's father."

Nhamo cast her eyes at Sam again.

Sam nodded thoughtfully. "She's right. It now dawns on me. He really killed my father." Tears ran down his cheeks.

"Thanks, Mama. Goodbye." She pressed a button and ended the conversation. She moved close to her husband and rubbed off his tears. "Sorry." She hugged him.

The following day, at work, Nhamo encountered Sergeant Zhira. "What a coincidence!" She stood in front of him, astonished. "What are you doing in Masvingo all the way from Mash Central?"

"It's a transfer. Who're you? Sorry, I've lost my memory."

"I'm Nhamo Chihera. You helped me with the money I used to photocopy my documents." She paused a little, but the sergeant still looked confused. "At Glendale Police Station."

"Well." They shook hands. "I remember now. The day you applied for this job, right?"

"That's right." A grin expression was on her face. "Give me your cellphone number, sir."

He gave it to her. "I need yours, too."

"It's ok." She gave it to him. "Do you work here?"

"Yes."

"I'm glad we're workmates."

"Me too."

After discussing a little, they parted ways with each other. As Nhamo walked home, a taxi stopped for her. She recognised the driver. He was the one whose car she had hired the previous day.

"Get in, Madam."

"Thank you." She got in.

"Do you remember me?" he asked with a grin.

"How can I forget a person I spent hours with yesterday? How're you?" she said amicably.

"I'm fine. I thought you wouldn't recognise me because of this new car of mine. I have five of them and a house."

"My memory is not that poor," she said, shaking her head.

"That's great."

Minutes later, she reached her destination. "Thank you for the lift."

"Don't mention it, Madam. I'll carry you almost every day."

"Thank you so much." She walked away.

"Let's keep in touch." He drove away.

Time flew. Nhamo and Sam had now stayed in Masvingo for a year and some months. They did not have a child yet—no sign of pregnancy at all.

"Who has a problem between you and your husband, Nhamo?" Beauty, Nhamo's workmate, asked as they were in the charge office at a police base. "You see me? I've got two girls I call my own daughters, although they've different fathers."

"Children come from God, my friend," Nhamo said. "If He doesn't want to give me, should I fight Him?"

"It's the right time you should wake up, my friend. If you're barren, it's ok, but if you're not, don't point at God for your ignorance."

"So what can I do?"

"I know you have three good men proposing love to you right now: the taxi driver, Sergeant Zhira and that businessman from Harare, who once carried you in his car from Harare to Glendale. You just choose one of them to test your fertility."

"I don't want to disappoint Sam; he's the one who sent me to school. I was nothing, but he made me become something. So—"

"Get me right, Nhamo. I'm not saying divorce Sam. Just get him a baby before he goes out to test his fertility with another woman. Once a man tastes honey from outside, he's gone for good. Wake up; this is the other side of the world."

There was silence. Immediately, a certain woman entered the charge office, tears on her cheeks. That was the second time she was reporting the same case to police officers deployed at the base.

"He's done it again." She was sobbing.

Nhamo and Beauty looked at each other with confusion.

"I told you the matter last week in the evening."

"I'm sorry," Beauty said, "different police officers are deployed to work here every day. You didn't talk to us, but to other police officers.

"Anyway, you can tell us your story, as if it's a new one. Just in brief."

"My husband eloped with another woman because I'm barren. He's abusing me. I don't know what got into him. He was a good husband before this. Help me..."

Nhamo glanced at her friend. *You're right about it.* "Once a man tastes honey from outside, he's gone for good."

They gave her some counselling, and she left the charge office, satisfied.

"You see the coincidence?" Beauty asked.

"Yes. It's exactly the same with what you've been saying. I'll consider your advice on my situation."

CHAPTER 16

THREE months later, Nhamo and Sam's marriage became something else. It was no longer a thing to admire. Every day was a day of quarrels in their house.

One night, they lay facing opposite directions on their bed. Sam had tears watering his pillow. Nhamo had an angry face.

She turned and faced skywards. "I never expected such silly questions and statements from you, Sam: 'I'm surprised you've changed so suddenly. For three months, you've been acting so weirdly...no longer going out with me...coming home late.' This and that!

"Do you want me to carry you on my back everywhere I go, Sam? Are you my baby? Why don't you understand the nature of my job? Don't compare me with you; you're unemployed; no one supervises you!"

Sam asked again, "Who's responsible for this pregnancy?"

"You asked me this stupid question yesterday. Now, again." She paused for a moment. "Sam, if you're sick and tired of this marriage, pack your goods and go!"

"Do you remember I sent you to school, Nhamo?" He was sobbing. "Sure, I never expected you would change and behave like this."

"Another silly question! If you need a refund, I can apply for a loan and give you your *fucken* money!"

"Is it you, Nhamo?"

"If it's not me, then it's your dead mother! Why do you ask silly questions?"

Sam freaked and slapped her. She sprang up and pushed him away from the bed. He fell onto the floor and quickly stood up, foaming at the mouth. They confronted each other like fighting cocks.

"How dare you slap a police officer?" She pointed her shaking finger to him, as if she wanted to prod his left eye. "Let this be the first and last slap from you! This is domestic violence, Mister!

"Let me be open to you." She patted her stomach. "The person responsible for this pregnancy is Sergeant Zhira. Now that you know the truth, you're free to make your decision! Living with or without you is all the same; I'm taking care of myself!"

"Tomorrow, I'm leaving you."

"Goodbye in advance." She moved to a wardrobe and took her purse. From it, she plucked out banknotes and threw them at his feet. "Enough to take you to the farm!"

Sam picked up the money and pushed it into his pocket.

"Sarapavana bus leaves Masvingo at 4 a.m. Take advantage of it." She sneered.

"Let me pack my goods; I've to leave now." He took his bag.

"Good idea. Let me help you pack them fast." She motioned and opened the doors of the wardrobe. "The bus is at Mucheke Rank right now. Go and sleep on it."

"Thank you. God bless you." He was sobbing. "You've allowed the devil to control our marriage. You've permitted a strange spear held by a strange hand to divide our love. You'll regret."

"That's what you think. Get out with your silly riddles!"

He stepped out into the rain. His jaws shuddered, and goose pimples formed on his hands. He rubbed his palms and blew onto them.

There was much activity at Mucheke Rank. Vendors were selling their stuff on shop corridors. People were drinking and dancing. Police officers were patrolling. Ladies of the night were everywhere; one of them approached Sam and whispered: "Just a dollar for a short time," but he ignored her. Later on, another one came, but she quickly made a U-turn. He recognised her. That was Beauty, his wife's close friend.

Sam moved away and joined some men who had just made a big fire after the rain had left them with drenched clothes. Many surrounded it, although it was reeking of burnt plastics and card boxes.

Sarapavana bus hooted. Sam left the fire and boarded it. Within some minutes, the bus was full, and it departed from the rank.

Nhamo and Beauty reported for duty at the police base. They were only two, and they liked it that way.

"How was your time off, Nhamo?"

"Fine, Beauty. What about yours?"

"I spent mine making money in the nightclubs," she bragged. "I saw your husband two days ago. At night. At Mucheke Rank. Where was he going?"

"I kicked him away; he was asking too many questions: 'Who's responsible for this pregnancy?' This and that. 'You're coming home late.' A lot. Just imagine it."

"He was wearing soaked clothes," Beauty sympathised.

"I don't care about that." She sneered. "The day he left, the taxi driver visited my home and tasted sweet water from my well. The game was fantastic; I enjoyed it. The following day, it was Sergeant Zhira."

Beauty smiled. "You're now enjoying your freedom."

"True. But Zhira must marry me, although he has a wife already."

Beauty shook her head. "Don't do that. The love from men is much when you're not married to them. Once you're in marriage with them, they make you suffer."

Nhamo nodded thoughtfully.

"Don't live like a prisoner. Next time off, I want to take you around the nightclubs in Masvingo. You've to know what joy is and how extra money is made."

"Sounds interesting." She nodded. "I'm thinking of inviting the Harare businessman. What do you think about this?"

"That's a brilliant idea. He'll definitely take you to a hotel or an expensive lodge. Go ahead."

Nhamo grinned.

"If you treat him like a king, he'll treat you like a queen, and you'll make much money from him."

"Thank you."

A month later, the Harare businessman and Nhamo lay on an expensive bed in a hotel. Both of them were naked. She inspected his body as she ran her tender palms on it. He had rash on his buttocks, on his thighs and around his manhood.

"I need a protected game," she said, still caressing him.

"I need an unprotected one," he demanded.

She stopped romancing him. "Why?"

"You think I can travel all the way from Harare and pay you much money for a protected match?"

"Don't worry about the money; I'll return it to you. I—"

"Shut up! What about the other amount I used to book the hotel? Don't be stupid!"

Nhamo mused over it. The money was too much for sure. She rubbed off tears forming in her eyes.

The man sat up, pinned her to the mattress and forced her legs open. Nhamo sobbed as he mercilessly pounded on her.

In the morning, the man left her in the town of Masvingo and drove back to Harare.

At noon, Sergeant Zhira knocked on the door to Nhamo's room. No response came for him, so he intruded. He saw Nhamo lie flat on her bed. Beside her was a photo that absorbed Sergeant Zhira's mind. In it, there was a familiar lady with her cute baby. He wondered if Nhamo had stolen it from him.

How did the photo with my ex-side chick and my baby girl get into her hands? He motioned to touch it.

Nhamo opened her eyes.

He withdrew his hand. "How are you?"

She just managed a low voice.

"You're not feeling well, are you?"

She shook her head.

"What's the matter?" He sat on the bed.

"Fever."

"Sorry." He touched her cheeks with the back of his hand. Her temperature seemed normal. "Where did you get this photo?"

"It's my mother's."

Zhira's heart skipped. "Your mother's? What do you mean?"

"I was left with the photo when she died. Whenever I think of her, I see her in this photo." She now got the strength and sat up. "This baby girl is me."

There was already sweat on Sergeant Zhira's brow, and his hands were perspiring.

Nhamo noticed the panic with him. "What's wrong?"

"To tell you the truth, I've got a twin photo of this one at home. I got it from this woman you call your mother. I met her at Heyshot Farm in Glendale."

Nhamo gaped at him as he explained.

"She was sort of my wife, and I'm the father of this baby girl with her."

"My father!" She hugged him. "I've been looking for you, Daddy," she said, sobbing.

"Me too." He sobbed, too.

From the day Nhamo knew her father, she had been thinking of terminating the pregnancy: *I can't keep this pregnancy from my biological father.* She closed the door of her room and sat on the floor. Some minutes later, she reached for a 2ltr container she had got from Beauty the previous day. It contained herbs mixed with unclean water.

Sometime later, Nhamo's neighbours heard her moaning. When they entered her room, they saw that she was bleeding excessively from her womanhood. They hurried with her to Masvingo General Hospital. On their arrival, a nurse observed something and said, "I'm sorry, she's dead."

—The End—